ICKY RICKY 3

THE DEAD DISCO RACCOON

I AM AN ALIEN!

Written & illustrated by

MICHAEL REX

A STEPPING STONE BOOK™

Random House 🏠 New York

To John and Michelle, Two Radical Sheep!

Copyright © 2014 by Michael Rex

All rights reserved. Published in the United States by Random House Children's Books, a division of Random House LLC, a Penguin Random House Company, New York.

Random House and the colophon are registered trademarks and A Stepping Stone Book and the colophon are trademarks of Random House LLC.

Visit us on the Web!
SteppingStonesBooks.com
randomhouse.com/kids

Educators and librarians, for a variety of teaching tools, visit us at RHTeachersLibrarians.com

Library of Congress Cataloging-in-Publication Data
Rex, Michael, author, illustrator.
The dead disco raccoon / written and illustrated by Michael Rex.
p. cm. — (Icky Ricky ; #3)
"A Stepping Stone Book."
Summary: "Icky Ricky has a lot of explaining to do—why he cleaned a house with a leaf blower, why he's storing money in his armpit, and why he let a stuffed dead raccoon drive his soapbox car." —Provided by publisher.
ISBN 978-0-307-93171-9 (pbk.) — ISBN 978-0-375-97103-7 (lib. bdg.) — ISBN 978-0-307-97540-9 (ebook)
[1. Behavior—Fiction. 2. Humorous stories.] I. Title.
PZ7.R32875Ded 2014 [E]—dc23 2013022708

Printed in the United States of America

10 9 8 7 6 5 4 3 2 1

Random House Children's Books supports the First Amendment and celebrates the right to read.

CONTENTS

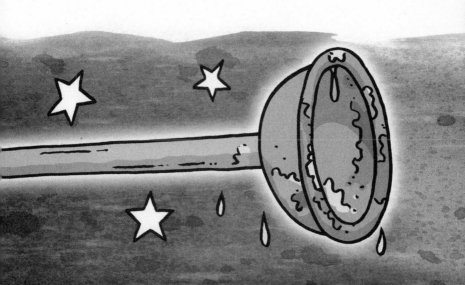

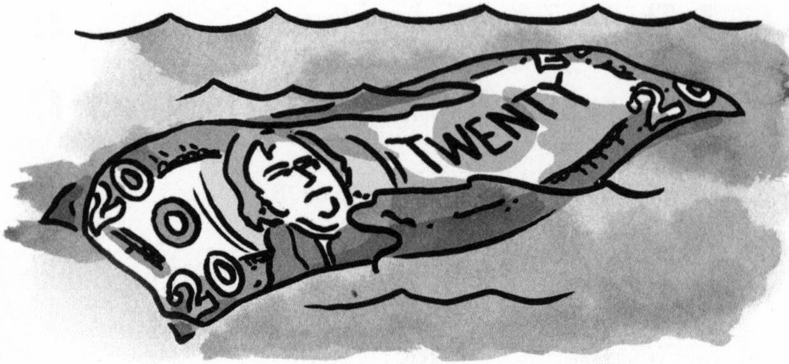
TWENTY
20
20
20

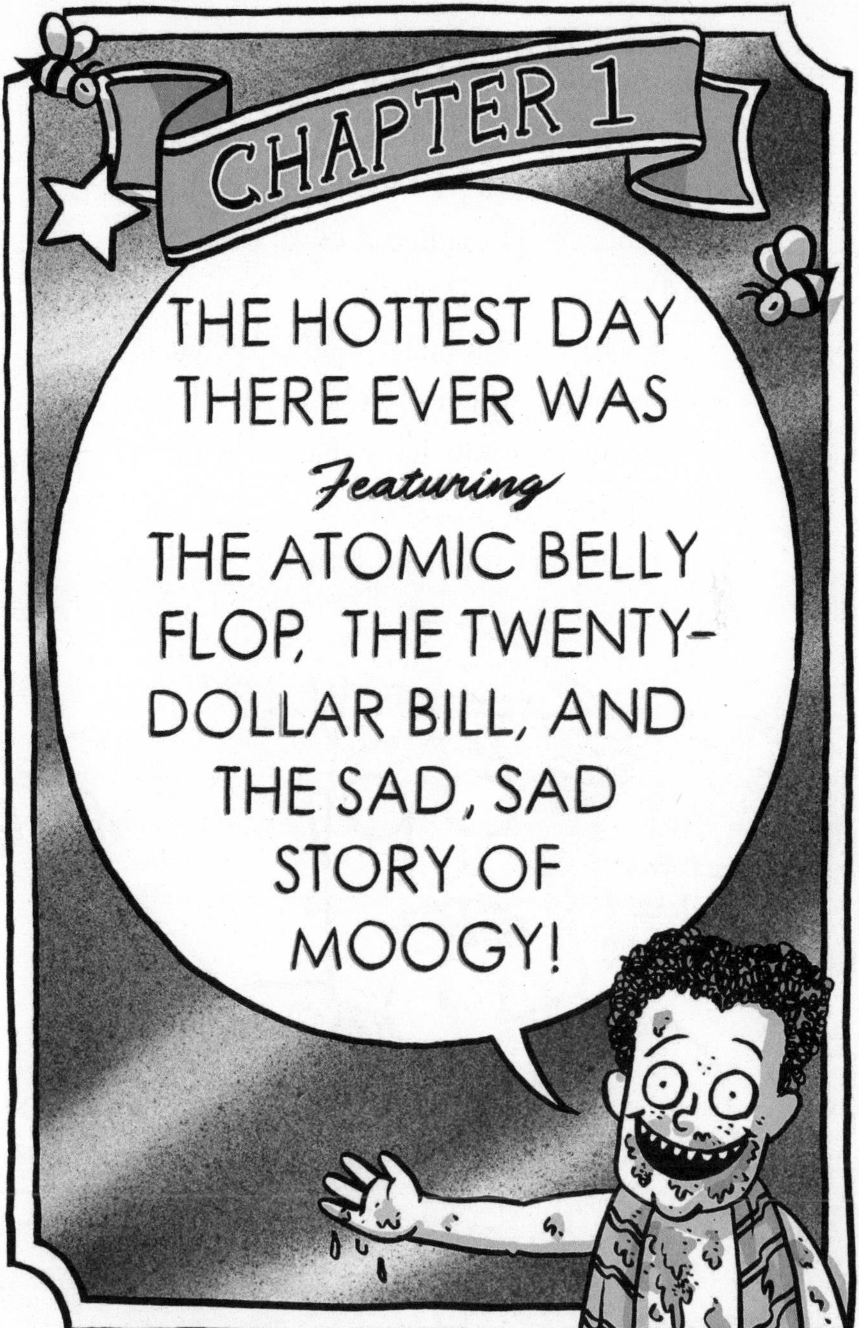
CHAPTER 1
THE HOTTEST DAY THERE EVER WAS
Featuring
THE ATOMIC BELLY FLOP, THE TWENTY-DOLLAR BILL, AND THE SAD, SAD STORY OF MOOGY!

TWEEEEEEEEEET! went the lifeguard's whistle at the town pool.

"Freeze!" said the lifeguard. "Who's under here?" He pulled a towel off a boy's head. It was Icky Ricky.

"Ricky!" the lifeguard said. "What the heck is going on here? Why is your towel on your head, and what's that brown stuff all over you?"

"It's ice cream," said Ricky.

"Why do you have ice cream all over you?" asked the lifeguard.

"Oh," said Ricky, "that's because no one loves Moogy!"

"Who?" asked the lifeguard.

"Moogy," said Ricky. "Nobody loves him. It's really sad."

"Ricky," said the lifeguard, "talk to me in plain English."

"Sure," said Ricky. . . .

It all started this morning. It was, like, one hundred degrees out, so Gus and Stew met me at the pool.

First we had a diving contest. Gus did a wicked Atomic Belly Flop. It was awesome.

Stew did a Triple Booyah. That's where
you yell "booyah!" while spinning three times.

I did my famous Backward Electrocuted-
Man Flip.

Then we remembered what day it was! It was the day we could see if we could get our twenty-dollar bill back. We had found twenty dollars in the pool and took it to the lost and found. They said if no one asked for it in three weeks, we could have it. And the three weeks were over today. No one had come for it, so they gave us the money!

"What are we going to spend the
money on?" asked Gus.

"A scuba suit?" said Stew.

"A helicopter?" said Gus.

But then I said, "Dudes. It's only twenty
dollars." Then I had my best idea of the
day. "Who wants to go to Cool Monkey for
ice cream?"

Stew and Gus were like, "Yes!"

Then I asked where we should put the money to keep it safe.

"Just put it in your pocket," said Stew.

I told them that my bathing suit didn't have any pockets. None of us had pockets.

"I don't want to lose it. We need to put it someplace really, really safe," I said. "Someplace so horrible, no one would dare steal it."

"What about your armpit?" said Stew. We laughed.

"Yeah! Your armpit!" Gus said. "It's all stinky and sweaty and only you would put your hand in there!"

"Yes!" I said. "The Armpit Bank! No one would steal it from there! But which armpit should I use?"

Gus said, "Let's see which one is worse."

I lifted my arms. Gus and Stew smelled my left pit and my right pit.

"They're about the same," said Stew.

"Okay!" I said. "Then I'll use my right armpit."

I folded up the twenty-dollar bill and stuck it in my armpit. Then I pressed my arm tight against my body to keep the money safe. When I raised my arm, it stayed there. I guess the sweat was kind of like glue or something.

It was almost noon, and the sun was right above us. We left the pool and ran to Cool Monkey. It was freezing inside. The air conditioner must have been on, like, one hundred degrees below zero.

I was looking at all the ice cream flavors. Then I saw a big, giant ice cream cake. It said "Happy Birthday, Moogy!" on it. I asked the girl who worked there why they were selling a birthday cake that already had a name on it. She told us that someone had ordered it but never picked it up.

"Poor Moogy," I said.

"Yeah," said Gus, "I wonder why Moogy never got his cake."

"Moogy could be a girl," said Stew.

"Nah," I said. " 'Moogy' is written in blue. He's a boy."

"He's a boy who had a really cruddy birthday," said Gus. "Because nobody picked up his cake."

"Maybe he was a really bad kid," I said. "Like he lit matches and swore all the time."

"Or maybe he rolled a bowling ball down a street," said Gus.

"Or he put a weasel in someone's car," said Stew.

"Maybe," I said, "he's really mean and smashed stuff."

"Yeah, like pumpkins at Halloween!" said Gus.

"And snowmen in the winter!" said Stew.

Then we all started laughing, and the girl was like, "Do you want to buy it?"

I said, "Buy what?"

"Duh, the cake," she said, and we all kept laughing. "It's only fifteen dollars."

We all said "yes" at once!

I peeled the twenty-dollar bill from the Armpit Bank and gave it to the girl. She made a really odd face and held it away from her like a stinky diaper.

We took the cake and went outside.
We were going to sit down and eat it right
there, but I said that it was a huge cake.
And that maybe we should share it with
everyone at the pool. Gus and Stew said
that was an awesome idea, so we headed
back to the pool.

It was really, really hot. We were
sweating like pigs just walking down the
street. Then the cake started to melt. We
walked faster. The ice cream dripped out of
the box and down my arm.

I was like, "Guys! We're not going to get to the pool before this melts. We need to eat it now."

They agreed. We had forgotten to ask for spoons, so we just started grabbing chunks with our hands and stuffing them in our mouths.

The ice cream was squishy and melty and running all over us. It dripped and oozed down our bodies. A big piece fell on the ground, but I picked it up and ate it. It was only in the dirt for four seconds, so I didn't break the five-second rule.

A bee started buzzing around us. Then another and another. They tried to land on us and eat the ice cream.

I told Gus and Stew to stand still. "Don't swat at the bees," I said. "They only sting if they get angry."

More bees and some other bugs came. So we stood there, frozen, for like a half hour. A group of older kids walked by. They pointed at us and started laughing.

"Hey, Gus, does this remind you of the day we met?" I whispered.

"Yeah, it does," said Gus.

"What happened?" asked Stew.

"I'll tell you about it some other time," I whispered.

The older kids walked away, still laughing.

"We can't just stand here all day," Stew whispered.

"Yeah, let's walk to the pool, very slowly," whispered Gus.

I said, "Yeah, baby steps," in my quietest voice.

So we walked the rest of the way in slow motion.

"You know," I whispered, "maybe Moogy wasn't a bad kid. Maybe something just went wrong on the day of his birthday. Maybe he had no friends to come to the party."

"Or maybe his parents didn't have enough money to get the cake," said Gus.

"Or they forgot where the ice cream store was," said Stew.

Then I said, "Or they forgot they ordered the cake."

We kept coming up with more reasons. Maybe his parents just forgot to pick the cake up or maybe they forgot it was his birthday or maybe they forgot they even had a kid.

"Man," Gus said, "Moogy's parents are lame."

"Poor little kid," said Stew.

I was getting really sad thinking about Moogy.

Stew said, "Are you crying?"

I said, "No way! I've just got ice cream in my eyes."

"I'm not crying, either," said Stew. "It's just ice cream."

Gus admitted that some ice cream had gotten in his eyes, too. We started to rub the ice cream out of our eyes. The bees got mad and buzzed again. We forgot to stay still and swung our arms all over. Then we saw we were close to the pool.

We ran really fast. Some of the bees and bugs followed us. We threw our towels over our heads and kept going. And then I had my best idea of the day!

"Guys! When we get to the pool, jump right into the water!" I screamed. "The bees and bugs will go away, and we'll clean the ice cream off!"

We ran as fast as we could through the entrance and right to the pool! Then all of a sudden, we heard a whistle blow, and someone yelled, "ADULT SWIM! All kids out of the pool!"

We were like, "Ahhhh!"
"To the showers!" I yelled.

We ran to the bathroom. We thought
we were going into the men's bathroom.
But since we had towels over our heads, we
ran into the women's bathroom by mistake
and people were screaming and stuff.

A lady threw a roll of toilet paper at us. We turned around and ran out. Then we ran through the sandbox, under the Ping-Pong table, and across the shuffleboard lanes!

"And that's when you stopped us," Ricky said. "You see? It all makes sense!"

"Um . . . yeah," said the lifeguard. "It makes *total* sense. I'm glad you didn't jump into the pool with all that ice cream on you."

"Yeah," said Ricky. "It would have been a major waste."

"Now go to the showers in the men's room and get cleaned up before you go swimming," said the lifeguard.

"Sure," said Ricky. He ran his finger across his belly and scooped up a blob of melted mess. "But first I'm going to have some more ice cream!"

ICKY RICKY'S POETRY CHILL BREAK #1

LIMERICKS

Don't tell anyone, but I like poems. Not the mushy kind where you talk about how your heart feels while watching a sunset, but cool ones. I like limericks because they are funny.

> There once was a kid named Gus.
> He made arm farts on the bus.
> On his hand he spit,
> Put his palm in his pit,
> And the sound, it created a fuss!

There once was a dude named Stew.
He had something brown on his shoe.
It turned out to be dirt,
So out loud he did blurt,
"Good thing it's not doggy doo!"

I once knew a boy named Ricky.
Everything he touched was sticky.
His pockets dripped slop.
His sneakers oozed glop.
And sometimes his nose he did picky!

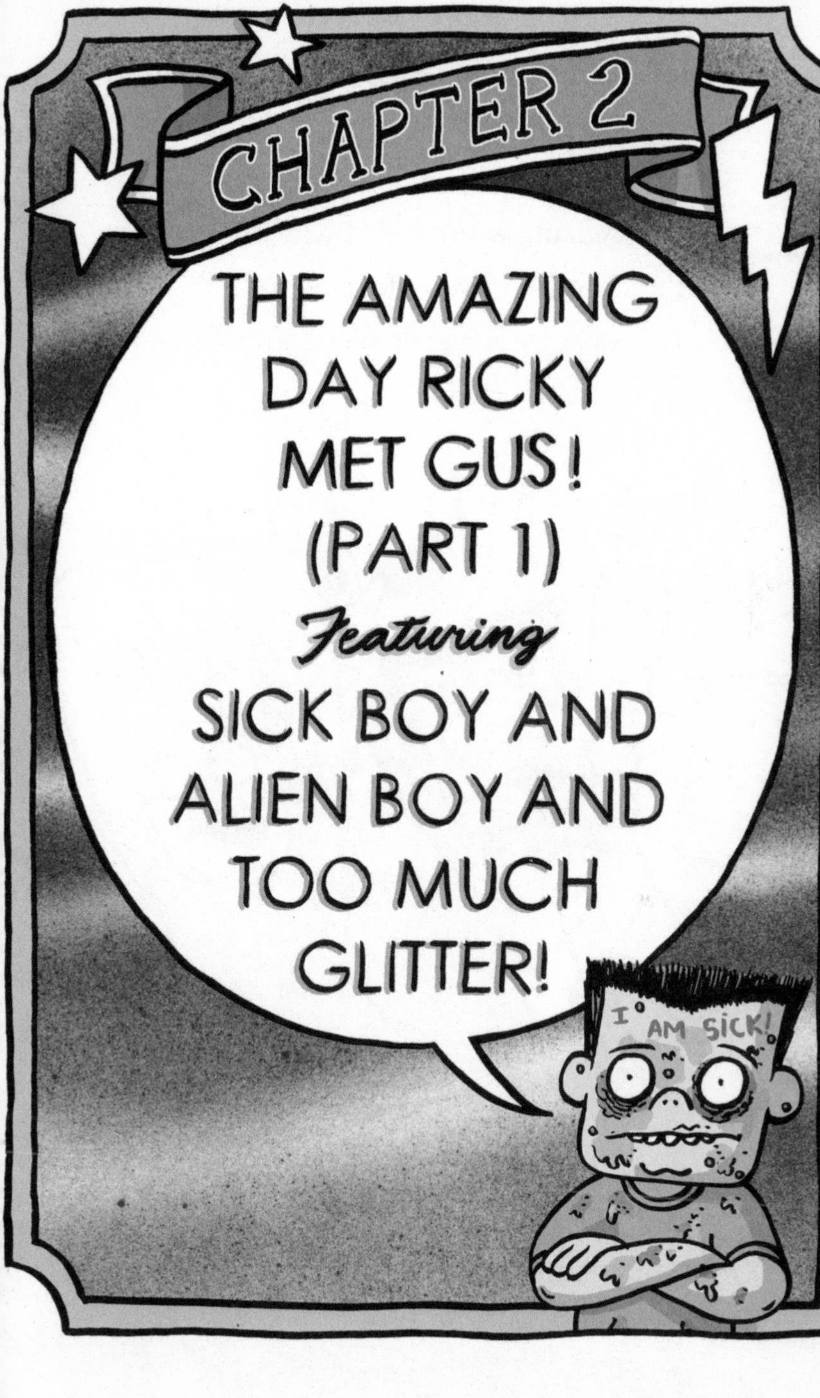
CHAPTER 2
THE AMAZING DAY RICKY MET GUS! (PART 1)
Featuring
SICK BOY AND ALIEN BOY AND TOO MUCH GLITTER!
I AM SICK!

"Ricky!" shouted his teacher, Ms. Jay, as he and Gus ran out the door of the school. "Where have you been?" she asked. "Why are you wearing a tutu, and why does it say 'I am an alien!' on your forehead?"

"Because we never learned any Toilet Magic!" said Ricky.

"I have no idea what that means," she said. "What have you done to Gus? It's his first day here! Why does it say 'I am sick!' on his head?"

Gus looked very worried, but Ricky started to explain everything.

"It happened like this," said Ricky. . . .

It all started during Mr. Kane's art class. Gus was sitting at my table and not really saying anything. He looked sad, so I tried talking to him.

I said, "How does it feel to be the new kid? Do you like it here?" He didn't answer. He was painting a guy break-dancing.

"Are you a good dancer?" I asked.

"I guess," said Gus quietly. He stared at his paper.

Then I said, "You'll like this school. It's pretty fun here, once you get to know people. My name is Ricky."

Gus finally looked up at me. "Ms. Jay says I have to stand up and talk to everyone in class," he said. "I have to tell them something about myself. I hate getting up in front of people and doing stuff."

"Why?" I asked.

He leaned in close and said, "Everyone will laugh at me."

"No, they won't," I said. "No one in class is *that* mean."

"I bet they will laugh," said Gus. "I'm really scared. I can't do it. I feel sick."

"You don't look sick," I said. And then I had my best idea of the day.

"If you want to look sick, you should be green," I said, and pointed at the paint in front of us.

Gus took his paintbrush and wiped
green paint on his cheek. He grinned. I put
some paint on his other cheek.

"You need dark circles under your
eyes," I said. I painted blue around his eyes.
He started laughing a bit.

"You need spots, too." I made red spots
all over the green paint.

"Stop it, you mean alien!" he said.

He picked up his brush again and smeared gray paint all over my face.

"You need to be foaming at the mouth!" I said. I painted white around his lips.

Gus was like, "Go back to outer space!"
He blew glitter onto my face.

Then we went kind of nuts. I poured
glue on his head and sprinkled on some
glitter. He glued two pencils to my hair.
I took a marker and wrote "I am sick!" on
his forehead.

And he wrote "I am an alien!" on mine.
Gus was really laughing, so I knew he had
forgotten about the talk.

Then Mr. Kane saw what we were doing and was like, "Boys! Stop that this instant!" The rest of the class looked at us and was totally silent. Mr. Kane was really mad and said, "Alien boy and sick boy, go to the boys' room and clean yourselves up! Right now!"

He pointed at the door. We got up and left. Gus looked really upset.

"Great!" he said. "It's my first day here, I have to talk in front of everybody, and I'm in trouble. This day can't get any worse!"

TO BE CONTINUED . . .

(HAIR BALL)

CHAPTER 3

THE TERRIFYING CAT APOCALYPSE

Featuring

TODD THE CAT, FLOOR SLUDGE, AND THE INDOOR LEAF BLOWER!

"What the heck is happening here?"
shouted Ricky's dad as he opened the
kitchen door.

"WHAAAT?" shouted Ricky. "I can't
hear you! The leaf blower is too loud!"

"Then turn it off!" shouted his dad.
He stepped into the kitchen. Ricky turned
off the leaf blower.

"Ricky," said his dad slowly, "why do
you have a leaf blower inside?"

RRRMM!!

"Because I always recycle," said Ricky.
Ricky's dad gave him a look. Ricky
knew it meant he needed to explain
himself. . . .

Stew came over to play, but I told him I had a job to do. It was time to feed Mrs. Lambert's cats.

"Who's Mrs. Lambert?" asked Stew.

"She's a lady who lives down the street," I said. "She went away for the night, and she asked me to feed her cats."

So Stew and I went over to her house. She had left a key hidden under a rock.

Mrs. Lambert has seven cats. Honest. Their names are Sleepy, Dopey, Happy, Grumpy, Bashful, Sneezy, and Todd. Those are really weird names, right? I mean, except for Todd.

When we got inside her house, Stew
saw all the cat food cans on the kitchen
counter.

"Why do they each have a name written
on them?" he asked.

"Because each cat is on a special diet
and eats a different food," I told him.

Well, here's where things got messed up. We opened all the cans at once and threw the lids in the recycling, because I always recycle. Then we realized we didn't know which can went to which cat.

I said, "The cats will know what to eat." Stew said that sounded right.

So we put the cans on the floor. All the cats ran for this one can that must have tasted the best. They started fighting over it.

"Wow! It's like a wrestling match!"
I said.

Todd was the biggest cat, and he won.
He ate the food. All the other cats started
looking at us and meowing. We pushed the
rest of the open cans toward the cats, but
they didn't like them.

Then Stew was like, "Uh . . . what do we do now?"

I was like, "Um . . . Mrs. Lambert said I could put out some dry food, too."

So I got out the big bag of dry food. The cats were going bonkers and jumped up on me. I dropped the bag on the floor, and it ripped. The cats went crazy eating the food.

"Oh no!" I said.

"Wow! Look at them!" said Stew.
"They must have really been starving."

The cats crowded around us again, all meowing like mad. They cornered us.

MEOOOOWW!

"They're like zombies!" said Stew.
"They just won't stop!"

"Yeah." I giggled. "It's a cat apocalypse!"

"They've taken over!" said Stew. We started laughing some more.

Then I remembered something. "Mrs. Lambert said for a treat, I could give them some milk."

So I pushed past the cats and got the milk from the fridge. Todd, I swear, jumped up on the counter and leaped on my head! I dropped the milk, and it spilled

everywhere. It mixed with the dry food and got sludgy. The cats were eating and lapping up all the stuff from the floor.

"We gotta clean this up!" I said.

"Yeah," said Stew. "Let's find a broom."

We tried to get across the kitchen, but the cats were everywhere and it was all slippery. Stew fell, then grabbed me. I went down right into some slop! The cats began licking the gunk off my face.

I got up and stepped right onto the litter box. The whole tray flipped over, flinging litter and cat poops across the floor. Then one cat started making this horrible sound, like *huuwaaaackssss, huuwaaaackssss,* and spit up a hair ball right onto Stew.

I found a broom in a closet and tried to sweep up the food and milk and litter and poops.

"This isn't working," I said. "It's too wet. We need a mop!"

Stew grabbed a mop and started using that. One cat thought the mop was a toy and attacked it.

"This isn't working, either," he said.
"We need something stronger!"

"Like what?" I said.

"I don't know, maybe a shovel?" he said.

Then I had my best idea of the day.

"What about a leaf blower?"

"You can't use them inside!" said Stew.

"Why not?" I said.

"You just can't!" said Stew.

"We've gotta try something! You stay
here and watch the cats!" I shouted as I ran
out the door.

I ran home, grabbed the leaf blower, and ran back. I plugged it in and turned it on!

The cats went nuts looking for places to hide. They kept banging into each other and leaping through the air.

The leaf blower pushed all the gunk
that was on the floor into one corner of the
kitchen. It formed this huge ball of soggy
food and milk and litter and poops. Stew
shoved it along with the mop like a hockey
puck. We blew it right out the back door
and into a garbage can!

"GOAL!" we cheered.

BRRRMMMM!!

Then I went back into the kitchen, and by accident I pointed the leaf blower at the little kitchen table. It blew the pile of paper napkins and a newspaper all over the room. But then I figured something out. If I held the leaf blower just right, I could keep the papers in the air. The cats started jumping and batting at the napkins.

Stew said, "Keep doing that. They like it!" So I kept blowing the napkins all over. Mrs. Lambert had also asked me to play with the cats a bit so they got some exercise. I guess that counted.

"And that's what happened," Ricky said.

"Well, I see you're trying to do the right thing," said Ricky's dad. "But you have to make sure this place looks like it did when you got here. You don't want Mrs. Lambert to be upset."

Ricky nodded. "We'll clean up the napkins and paper and stuff."

"Okay," said his dad. He looked at the leaf blower. "So, this thing cleans well?"

"Yeah," said Ricky, "it blew all the mess right out the door."

"I'm going to need that," his dad said as he took the leaf blower from Ricky.

"What for?" asked Ricky.

"I promised your mom I would clean the living room before she got home!"

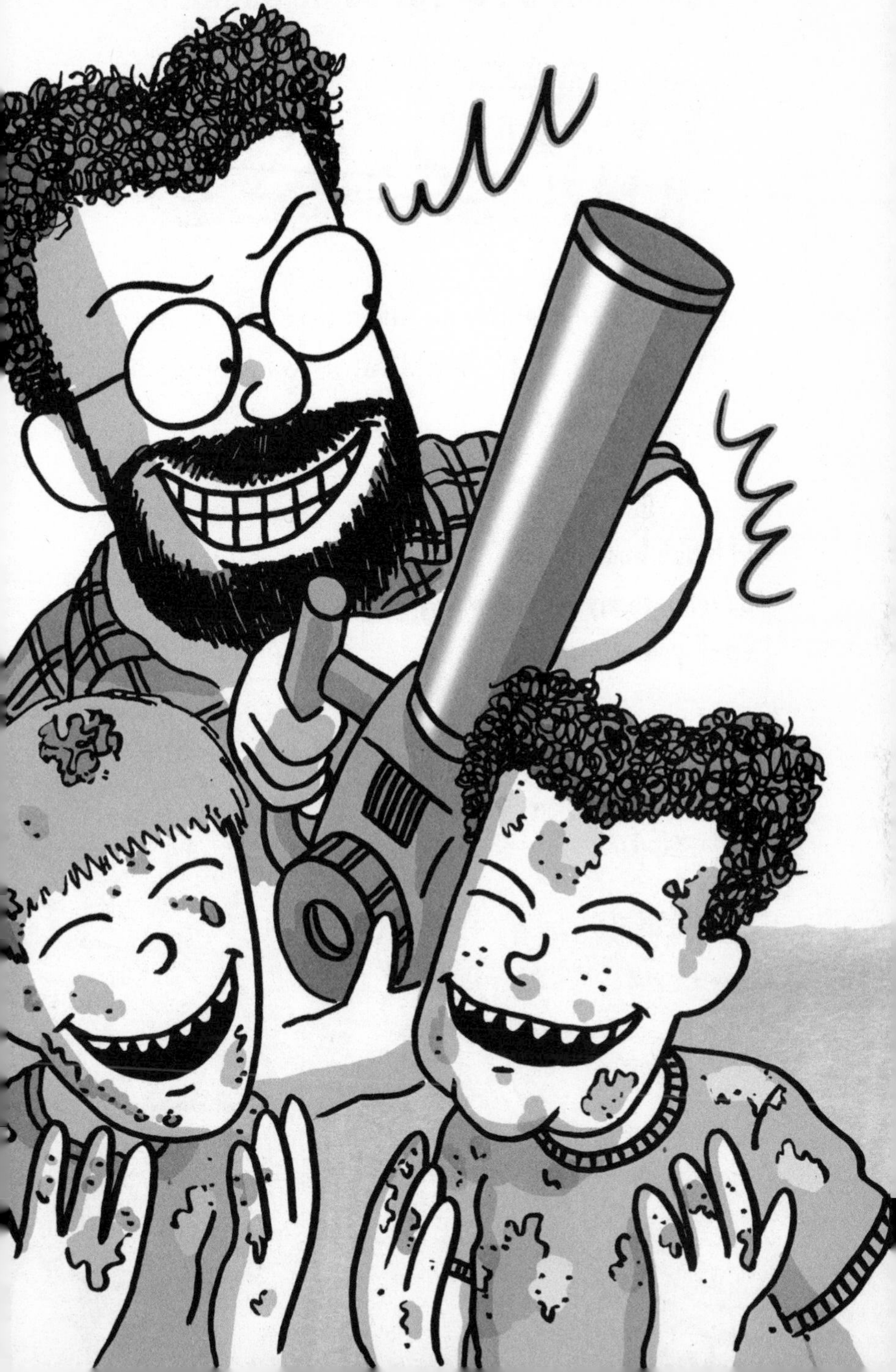

ICKY RICKY'S POETRY CHILL BREAK #2

Haiku are usually about nature and beauty. Anything can be beautiful if you look at it the right way.

Old black banana
Underneath my bedroom rug
I smell you at night

Puddle of thick mud
I jump in and swim around
I am late for school

Moldy egg sandwich
I made you ten weeks ago
Forgot to eat you

A stink is drifting
Noses burn and eyes water
Tacos for dinner

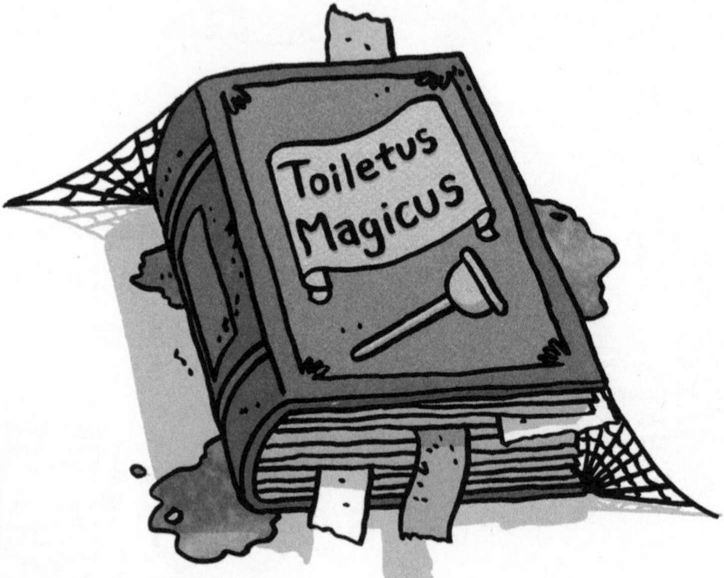
Toiletus
Magicus

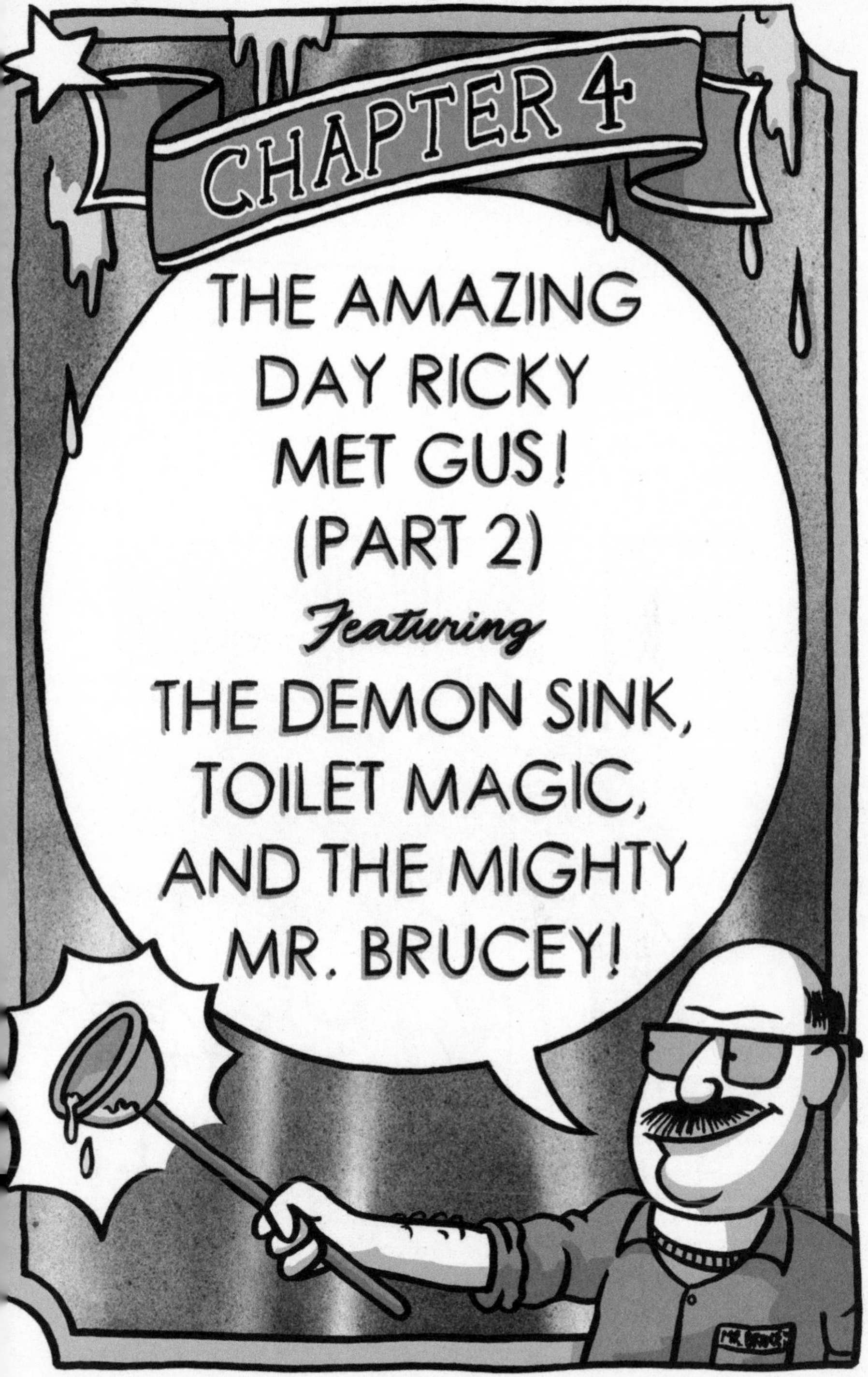
CHAPTER 4
THE AMAZING DAY RICKY MET GUS! (PART 2)
Featuring
THE DEMON SINK, TOILET MAGIC, AND THE MIGHTY MR. BRUCEY!

Ricky and Gus stood outside the school
with Ms. Jay. Gus was very worried.

"But why are you wearing a tutu?"
she asked.

"Oh yeah. I'll get to that," said Ricky,
and he kept talking. . . .

Gus and I walked to the bathroom. He was still upset.

I tried to turn on the water, but the sink handle hardly moved. There's only one sink in there, so we pushed and pushed the handle really hard. Finally, the handle turned, and the water came shooting out into the sink! It splashed back up and sprayed all over us.

"Curse you, demon sink!" I shouted.
Gus started laughing again. I reached over
to turn off the water, but the handle was
stuck. The water was going everywhere.

"We shall conquer you, demon sink!"
shouted Gus. "Prepare for battle!" He
grabbed the handle, too.

"This is the end for you!" I said.

We pulled together and shut it off. We
were soaked. And the paint and glitter that
had been on our faces and hair had mixed
with the water. It was all over the sink and

the floor. The marker on our foreheads hadn't washed off, though.

We yanked paper towels from the paper towel thing and wiped everything up. We threw the towels away, but there was only a teeny, tiny little garbage can. We filled that up really fast. We had tons of wet, sloppy paper towels left.

Gus said, "What are we going to do with all these?"

Then I was like, "Well, we can flush them." So we finished cleaning ourselves and the sink and the floor. We chucked all the paper towels into the toilet, which, come to think of it, wasn't a good idea. Because when we flushed it, it gurgled and made all these weird noises.

GLURRRRRPFF!
GLUFG!

"Oh no!" I said. "The demon sink has a demon toilet brother!"

The water started coming up instead of going down, and it poured over the sides of the toilet.

I was freaking out. "How do we stop it? How do we stop it?"

"At home we jiggle the handle!" shouted Gus.

I jiggled the handle, but the toilet just flushed again.

"That didn't work! What now?" I said.

Then Gus was like, "I don't know! How about magic?"

I didn't know if he was serious or not, but my mom always said I should try new things. So I said, "Okay!"

I pointed my hands at the toilet like I was casting a spell.

Gus was laughing really hard. "That was the worst demon toilet spell I ever heard!"

I was laughing, too. "I didn't get much time to practice. Can you do better?"

Gus held his hands up and said:

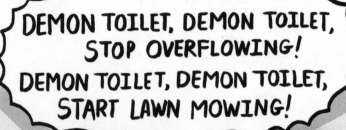

DEMON TOILET, DEMON TOILET, STOP OVERFLOWING! DEMON TOILET, DEMON TOILET, START LAWN MOWING!

"That was terrible!" I said. "Lawn mowing? Really?"

Gus said, "It was the only rhyme I could think of!"

We started laughing really hard again, and I slipped and fell into Gus. Then he slipped, too.

Water, paper towels, and paper towels with paint, glitter, and glue on them were floating all over the floor!

Gus stopped laughing. He looked really worried again. "Oh no! Now we are really going to get in trouble!"

Then I heard the best sound in the world. You know how Mr. Brucey, the custodian, is always whistling? Well, I heard him whistling, so I said to Gus, "Stay here! I'm going for help!"

I ran out of the bathroom and shouted, "Help! The toilet is overflowing!"

Mr. Brucey saw me and grabbed his plunger. We both ran into the bathroom. Gus had climbed up on the sink now.

Mr. Brucey was like:

WELL, SPANK ME TILL I'M CROSS-EYED!

I didn't know what that meant, but he went right to work on the demon toilet! And you know what? It was amazing. You know how Thor has his hammer? And he can do all sorts of amazing stuff with it?

Well, Mr. Brucey has a plunger, and he used that plunger in ways I never imagined. He was pushing and pulling and swinging and shoving it back and forth. He even hit the toilet with it and started saying words I didn't know!

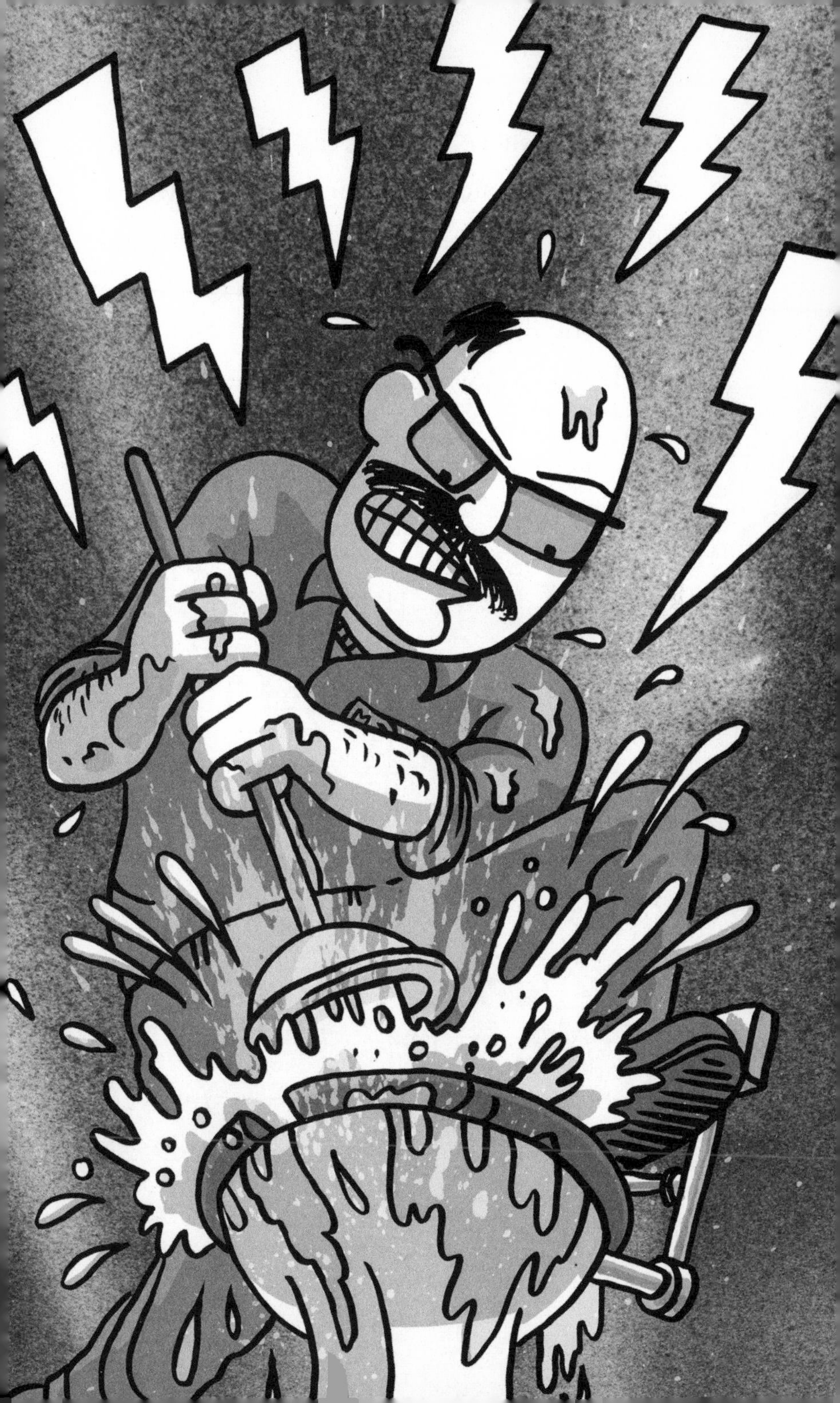

Finally, there was this big burping sound, and the water stopped. The bathroom was a mess. Our clothes were soaked. Mr. Brucey, who is usually a real nice guy, had sort of a mean look on his face.

He said, "Boys, go to the principal's office."

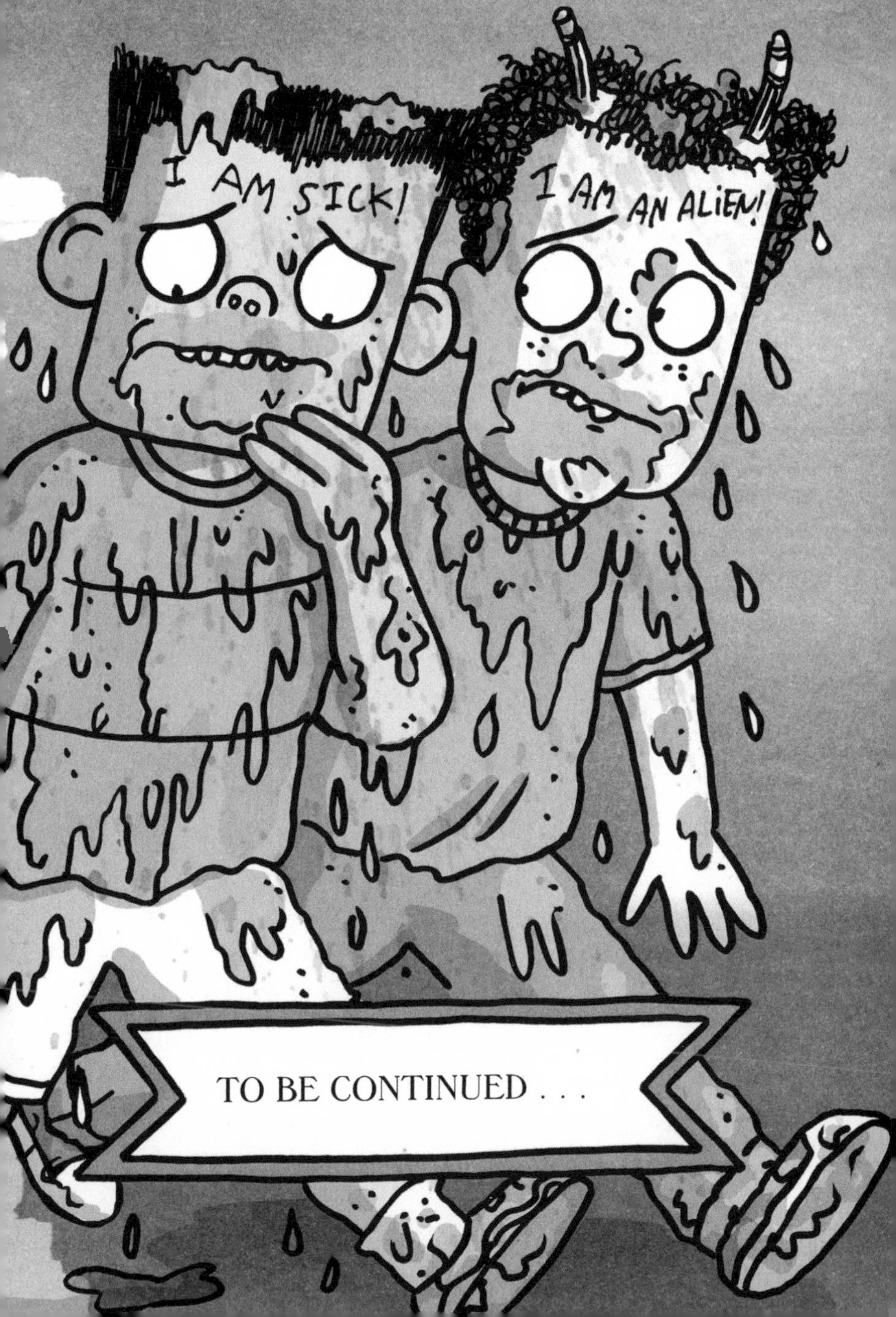
I AM SICK!
I AM AN ALIEN!

TO BE CONTINUED . . .

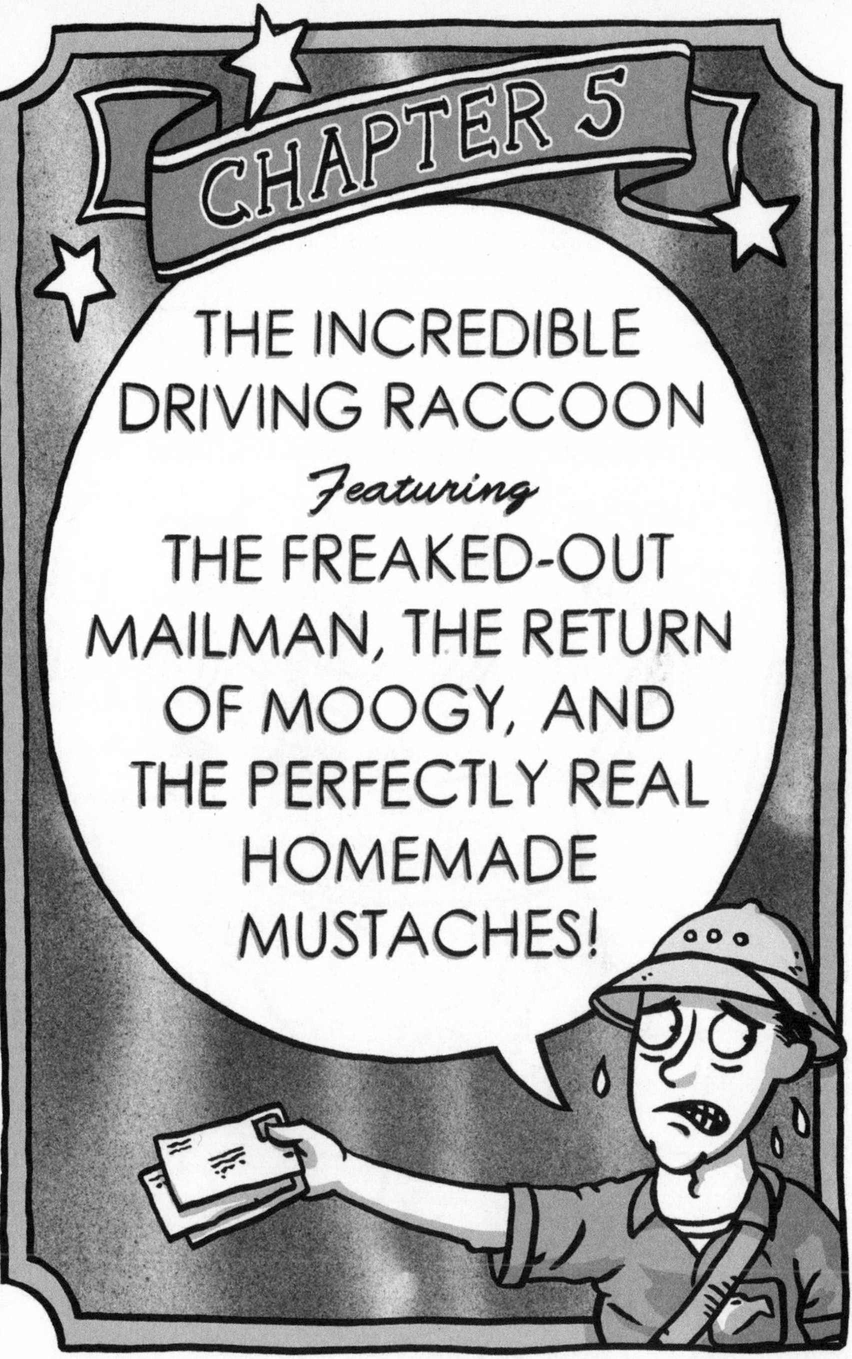
CHAPTER 5
THE INCREDIBLE DRIVING RACCOON
Featuring
THE FREAKED-OUT MAILMAN, THE RETURN OF MOOGY, AND THE PERFECTLY REAL HOMEMADE MUSTACHES!

"Yikes!" said the mailman as he stumbled out of his mail truck, spilling letters and magazines all over the ground. He was shaking, and his eyes bugged out. Ricky, Gus, and Stew ran up to him.

"What in the world is going on?" the mailman asked. "And why do you all have fake mustaches?"

"Because the garage sale was all lady
stuff," said Ricky.

"What are you talking about, kid?"
asked the mailman.

"Well," said Ricky, "this is the way it
happened. . . ."

It all started when Stew and Gus and I went to this garage sale. There were some ladies' hats, fancy dishes, old cookbooks, and this really big dollhouse. The dollhouse was kind of cool because if you stuck your head in a room, you felt like you were actually there.

And if someone put their eye to the
window from the other side, it looked like
a giant was peeking in!

It was a pretty lame garage sale, though.
There really wasn't anything for boys. But
then I was like, "OMG! What is that?" And
I pointed at the most amazing thing ever!

It was some sort of frozen raccoon!

"Is that a real raccoon?" asked Gus.

"It looks real," said Stew.

A man came over. It was his garage sale.

He said, "It *is* real, but it died. Then it was stuffed and put on that display. That's called taxidermy."

I asked, "Why would you sell such an excellent thing?"

The man said, "My wife hates it. It freaks her out."

Gus asked, "How much is it? We have five dollars."

The man said, "It's twenty dollars."

Then a lady came up to the man, and it must have been his wife. She asked if we wanted the raccoon for five dollars, and we were like, "YES!" Then she looked at her husband with the stink eye. That's when you're mad at someone, but you don't want anyone else to know. But we knew.

Anyway, we bought the raccoon.
I picked it up to carry it home. It wasn't
heavy, but it was hard to grip. I asked Stew
to take the bottom, and I held the arms,
and we kept walking.

Gus asked, "What are we going to
name it?"

"Baboon," said Gus.

Stew and I went, "Huh?"

"Baboon the Raccoon. It rhymes,"
said Gus.

"Nah," said Stew. "He needs a regular
name, like Bill or Joe."

I said, "He needs a really cool name
like . . ."

Then, I swear, we all said "Moogy" at
the same time!

"Moogy the Raccoon! Awesome!" I said.

Just then, we heard a snap, and Moogy's arms fell off.

"Yikes!"

"Moogy!"

"We gotta fix him! Right away."

We picked up the pieces and ran home.

When we got there, Stew and Gus stayed outside, and I grabbed some stuff from my room, like tape and glue. Then I found a hammer and nails in the garage.

When I ran back to Stew and Gus, they were cracking up.

"Look," said Gus. "Disco Moogy." He held up Moogy's arms and made them point up and down. Then Gus was singing:

I grabbed the arms and said,
"Umpire Moogy!"

Stew grabbed the arms and shouted,
"Soldier Moogy!"

We couldn't stop laughing. But we realized that while we were playing with Moogy, his hair was starting to fall out. I picked up the tape and said, "Let's fix him!"

Stew held the arms in place, and I wrapped the tape around them. They were still wiggly, so I got the hammer. I put some nails in his shoulders to make the arms really tight.

There was hair all over the sidewalk. I took some tape and pushed the sticky side onto the hair.

Gus and Stew were like, "What are you doing?"

"Making a mustache!" I said, and I stuck the tape to my face.

Gus and Stew did the same. Mine was like a cowboy one. Gus made a real wide one that reached his ears, and Stew made one that's called a Fu Manchu.

They were the best raccoon-hair mustaches ever. We were looking at Moogy again, and Gus said, "He looks like he's driving a car!"

Gus was right. When we put him back together, we had pointed his arms straight forward.

"Yeah, he does!" I said, and then I had my best idea of the day. I ran to the garage and got out the soapbox car that I built in Kidscouts. It goes really fast. We put Moogy in the seat. His hands touched the steering wheel perfectly. Then we pushed

the car out into the middle of the street.
Good thing I live on a hill, because all we
had to do was give it a little shove, and it
took off! It started flying down the hill.

We ran after it. I know Moogy wasn't really steering, but the soapbox car was going perfectly straight. Moogy passed a mom who was walking a little girl in a stroller, and they both started screaming.

Then he passed a lady who was
watering her garden. And she started
screaming! It's like they'd never seen a
raccoon driving a soapbox car before.

And we were saying, "Sorry! Sorry! It's not a real raccoon!" But I don't think they cared.

The car was rolling like mad now. I swear it had to be going one hundred miles per hour! But then it hit a bump and swerved.

I was screaming, "Moogy! Drive straight! Drive straight!"

Gus and Stew started laughing really hard. "He can't hear you!" they said. "He's just a stuffed raccoon!"

"Yeah, and a terrible driver!" I said.

Moogy hit a tree and shot out of the car. He went flying through the air and into the big open door on the mail truck!

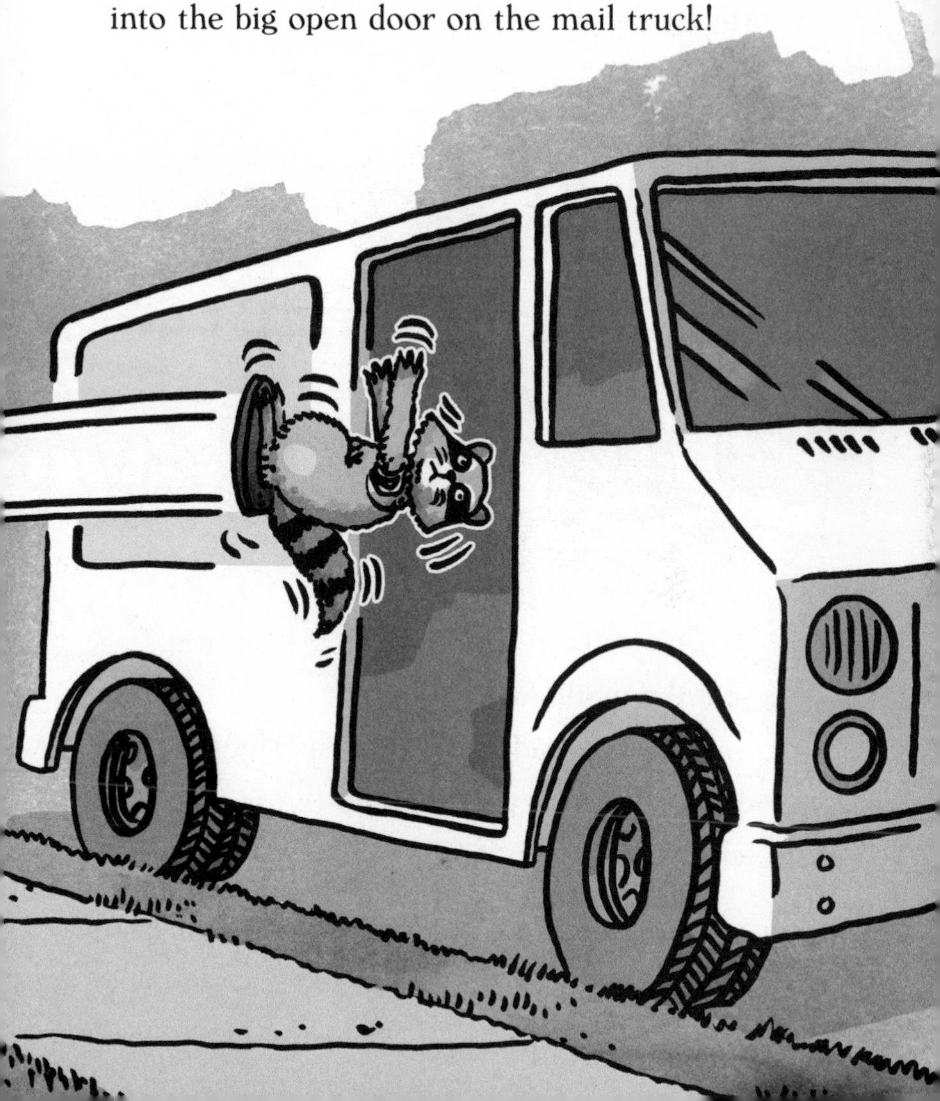

"That's when you got scared and ran out of the truck and spilled those letters all over the place!" Ricky told the mailman.

"I didn't get scared!" said the mailman. "I was surprised. There's a big difference." He reached into the truck and handed Moogy back to Ricky.

"Here, take this thing. It's disgusting," said the mailman.

"Sorry," said Ricky. He put Moogy down and started picking up the scattered letters. Gus and Stew picked some up, too.

"Don't worry about that," said the mailman. "I'll do it."

"But I feel kinda bad about the mess," said Ricky. "At least let us give you a hand."

"Yaaaah!" screamed the mailman as he looked into his mail satchel. "I think you already did!"

ICKY RICKY'S POETRY CHILL BREAK #3

ACROSTIC

This is a really easy kind of poem. Choose a subject, and use the letters in the word to describe the subject.

TOE CHEESE

Thick and warm
Oily and odd
Exotic and mysterious

Clump yanked free
Handy for crafts
Elastic-like and moldable
Entertaining for hours
Stiff when dried out
Exhibit my artwork

STEP 1: PICK

STEP 2: SCULPT

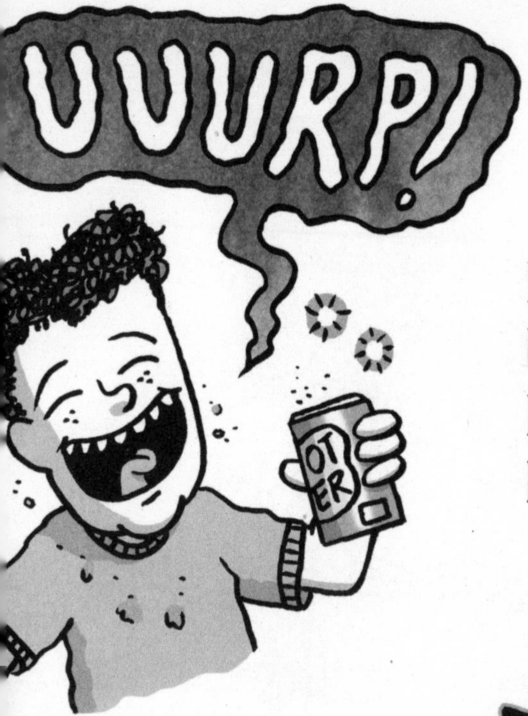
UUURP!
OT ER

BURP

Bigger is better
Underrated by adults
Root beer will help
Practice makes perfect

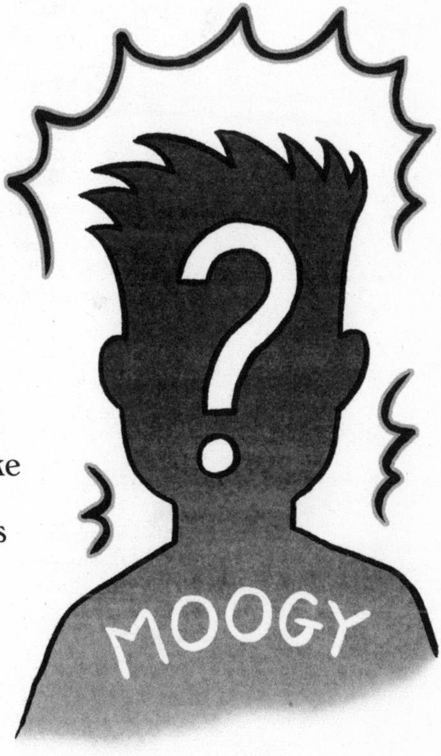
?
MOOGY

MOOGY

Mysterious person of mystery
One day I'd like to meet him
On his birthday he had no cake
Great at having rotten parents
Yeah! Moogy is the best!

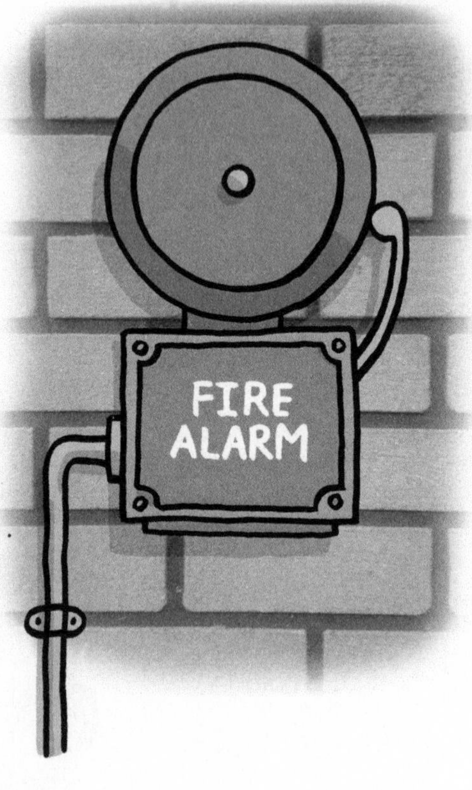
FIRE
ALARM

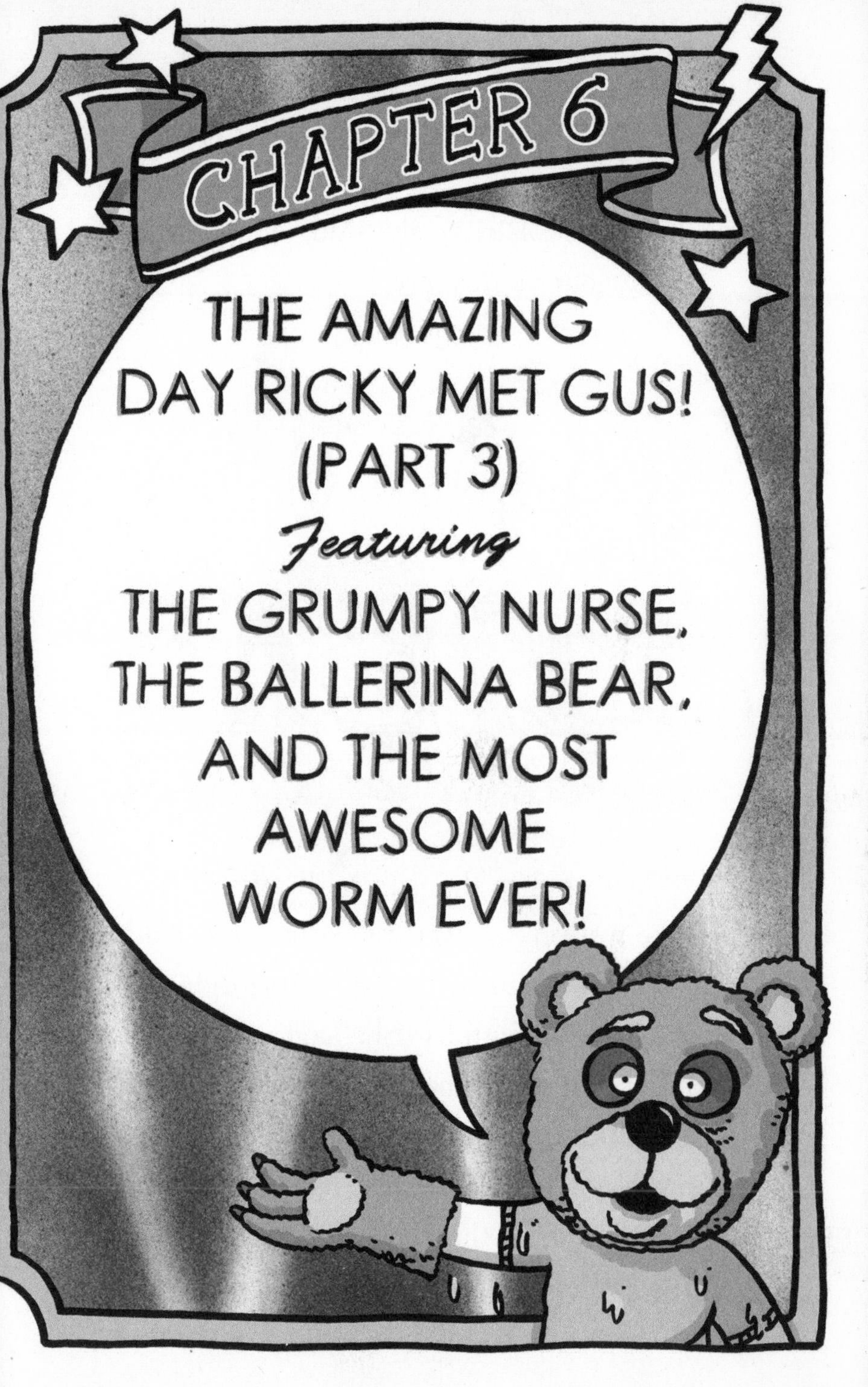
CHAPTER 6
THE AMAZING DAY RICKY MET GUS! (PART 3)
Featuring
THE GRUMPY NURSE, THE BALLERINA BEAR, AND THE MOST AWESOME WORM EVER!

Ms. Jay shook her head and did a face palm.

"Please, Ricky," she said, "just tell me where your clothes are."

"Sure . . . ," said Ricky.

We went to the principal's office. But since we were so wet, the secretaries said to go to the nurse. But the nurse didn't want to deal with us. She said to go to the principal's office. We went back, and they said to go to the nurse. We went back to the nurse, and she was real grumpy. She took us to the backstage area in the auditorium.

She said, "Here's a box of costumes. Find something in it and get out of those wet clothes." Then she left.

We took off our wet clothes and dug through the box. Gus pulled out the shirt and pants from a gangster costume and put them on.

"Great," he said. "Now I have to get up in front of everybody in these stupid clothes."

"They look pretty normal," I said.

"Everyone is going to laugh," said Gus.

"No, they won't," I said. I dug through the box. "This is all that's left." I held up a bear costume and ballerina costume.

"Which is better?" I asked. "The bear or the ballerina?"

That got Gus laughing again.

"Put them together," said Gus.

I put on the ballerina skirt, the bear mask, and the bear-claw gloves. Then I started dancing around and jumping and spinning and twirling. It was kind of hard to see out of the mask, but I kept going.

"I'm the ballerina bear, la, la, la, la, la.
First I will dance! Then I will eat you!"
I held my arms up and roared. I did some
more spins. I smashed into a wall and fell
down. All of a sudden, the fire alarm rang.
Gus and I looked at each other and said
"Fire drill!" at the same time.

I took off the bear mask and the
gloves, but I didn't have time to take the
skirt off. We ran out of the auditorium and
out the closest door.

"And that's when you found us!" Ricky
said.

Ms. Jay shook her head again. "Okay,
okay," she said.

"Do I still have to talk in front of
everybody?" asked Gus.

"Yes," said Ms. Jay. "But there won't be
time today. You can do it tomorrow. Just
get in line with the rest of the class."

In the field behind the school, each class had lined up quietly behind a teacher. They did this for every fire drill. Then everyone noticed Ricky was in a tutu. Kids started pointing. Some kids started laughing. Then more laughed. Soon three whole grades were laughing at Ricky. He just stood there in the tutu.

Gus jumped in front of Ricky. He
froze for a moment. Then he did a perfect
moonwalk. The kids stopped laughing at
Ricky. Gus started to dance, and the kids
clapped a beat. Gus did the robot. He
did the helicopter! He shuffled! Then he
jumped on the ground and did the worm.
He was amazing.

Some kid shouted out, "What's his name?" and then some other kid shouted, "It's Gus!" The kids were all chanting, "Gus! Gus! Gus!"

Gus turned his back on the crowd and looked at Ricky.

"I guess being in front of a crowd isn't too bad," he said. But Ricky hardly heard him over the cheers.

A little more . . .

The next day, Ricky and Gus got to school early so that they could give Mr. Brucey a drawing they made. Mr. Brucey really liked it.

They brought a drawing to Mr. Kane, too.

Mr. Kane looked at it. "Thank you," he said, but he didn't smile. "The mess you made is still over there. Clean it up and get to class."

Ricky and Gus wiped the paint off the table, cleaned the brushes, and put all the supplies back in place. Then they walked to the door.

"Hey, boys?" called Mr. Kane. They turned around to look at him.

"See you later in class, all right?" he said.

DON'T MISS THE NEXT EXCITING ICKY RICKY BOOK!

ICKY RICKY 4

THE HOLE TO CHINA

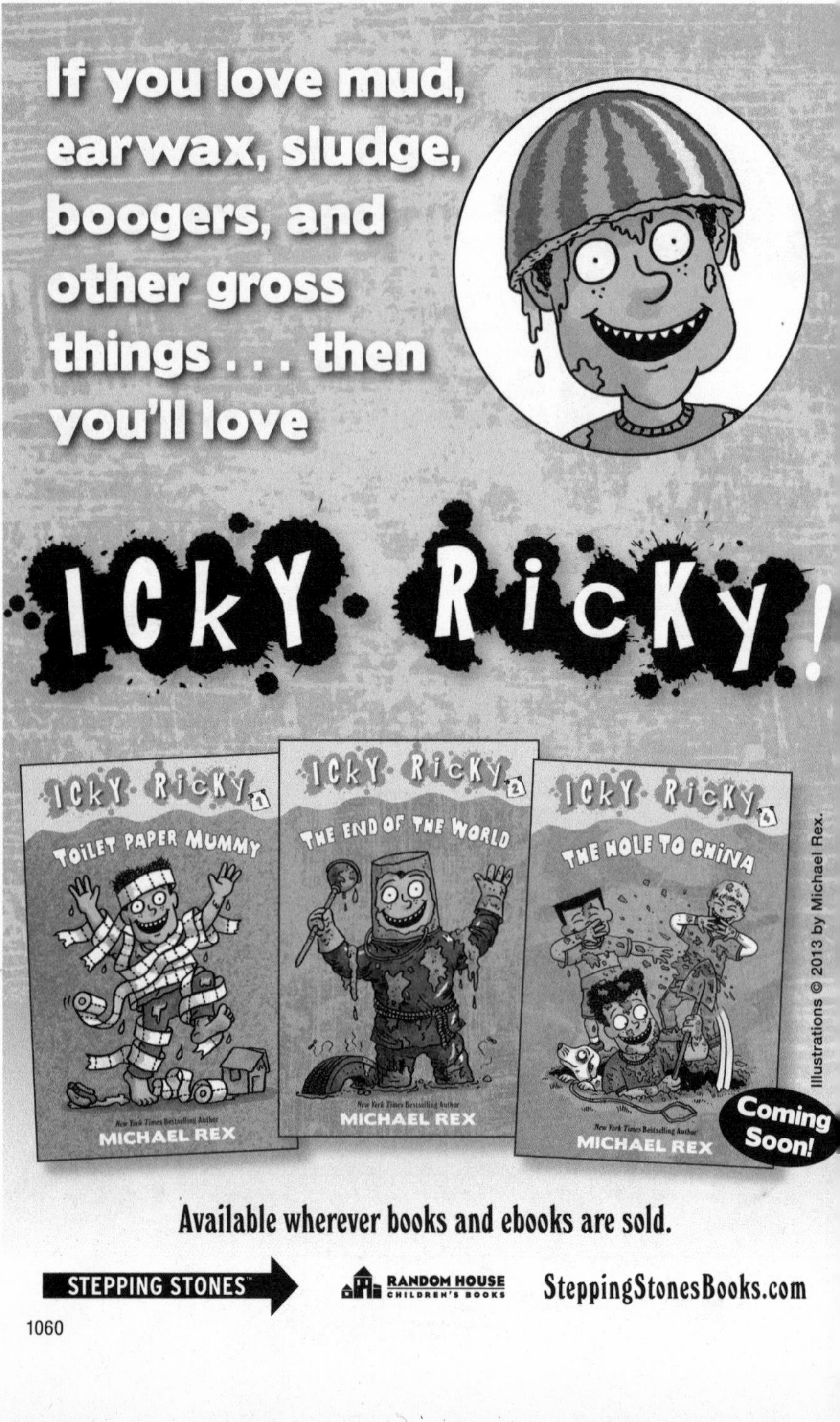
If you love mud, earwax, sludge, boogers, and other gross things . . . then you'll love
ICKY RICKY!
ICKY RICKY 1
TOILET PAPER MUMMY
New York Times Bestselling Author
MICHAEL REX
ICKY RICKY 2
THE END OF THE WORLD
New York Times Bestselling Author
MICHAEL REX
ICKY RICKY 4
THE HOLE TO CHINA
New York Times Bestselling Author
MICHAEL REX
Coming Soon!
Illustrations © 2013 by Michael Rex.
Available wherever books and ebooks are sold.
STEPPING STONES™
RANDOM HOUSE CHILDREN'S BOOKS
SteppingStonesBooks.com

1060